MR. FUNNY
upsets Mr. Fussy

Original concept by Roger Hargreaves
Illustrated and written by Adam Hargreaves

MR. MEN   LITTLE MISS

World International

Mr Funny lives in a teapot shaped house.

He drives a shoe shaped car.

And he has a teacup shaped bath.

Mr Fussy lives in a very ordinary house and drives a very ordinary car and his bath is a very ordinary bath.

Mr Funny is a very funny fellow.

So funny that when he pulls one of his funny faces you can't help but laugh.

Mr Fussy is very serious.

Very serious about keeping everything neat and tidy and spic and span.

Now Mr Funny lives at the very end of Long Lane and Mr Fussy lives half way down Long Lane.

So whenever Mr Funny goes out for a drive in his shoe car he has to pass by Mr Fussy's house.

Every time that Mr Funny passes Mr Fussy he pulls one of his funny faces.

And as hard as he tries, Mr Fussy can't help laughing.

He laughs so much that he ends up having accidents.

Like the time he was mowing his lawn.

He laughed so much he ruined all his nice straight lines.

And when he was cleaning his windows.

He laughed so much he fell off his ladder and squashed his prize pumpkin.

And he burnt his shoe laces while he was ironing them.

Mr Fussy was fed up.

But then he had an idea.

He put up a sign on the lane just before his house.

It read: 'Please Beep Your Horn'.

"That should work," he said to himself.

The idea was that if Mr Funny beeped his horn Mr Fussy would have some warning and he could stop whatever it was he was doing.

The next day Mr Funny was driving down the lane as usual when he saw Mr Fussy's sign.

So he beeped his car's horn and stopped his shoe car outside Mr Fussy's gate.

Mr Fussy had not reckoned on the sound that Mr Funny's car horn would make.

It doesn't go BEEP.

Oh no, it sounds like somebody making a very loud raspberry noise.

'THURRRPT!!' went the car horn.

Mr Fussy was outside in his coal bunker.
Stacking his coal in neat rows.

Mr Fussy didn't like untidy piles of coal!

When Mr Fussy heard the sound Mr Funny's car made he started to giggle.

And then he chuckled.

And then he laughed.

And he laughed so much he fell over into his neatly stacked coal.

Once he had recovered from his laughing fit he stormed out of his coal bunker.

He was covered from head to foot in coal.

And he was furious.

He stormed over to Mr Funny.

"That's the most ridiculous car horn I've ever heard," he yelled at Mr Funny.

"There's a reason for that," Mr Funny explained.

"It's because it's not a car horn,"

"It's a ...

... shoe-horn, ha ha ha, hee hee hee," he laughed.

And even Mr Fussy had to admit that was quite funny.

Wouldn't you agree?

• RETURN THIS WHOLE PAGE •

Join Our Club!

When you become a member of the fantastic Mr Men and Little Miss Club you'll receive a personal letter from Mr Happy and Little Miss Giggles, a club badge with your name, and a superb Welcome Pack (pictured below right).

You'll also get birthday and Christmas cards from the Mr Men and Little Misses, 2 newsletters crammed with special offers, privileges and news, and a copy of the 12 page Mr Men catalogue which includes great party ideas.

If it were on sale in the shops, the Welcome Pack alone might cost around £13. But a year's membership is just £9.99 (plus 73p postage) with a 14 day money-back guarantee if you are not delighted!

HOW TO APPLY To apply for any of these three great offers, ask an adult to complete the coupon below and send it with appropriate payment and tokens (where required) to: Mr Men Offers, PO Box 7, Manchester M19 2HD. Credit card orders for Club membership ONLY by telephone, please call: **01403 242727.**

To be completed by an adult

❏ **1.** Please send a poster and door hanger as selected overleaf. I enclose six tokens and a 50p coin for post (coin not required if you are also taking up 2. or 3. below).

❏ **2.** Please send ___ Mr Men Library case(s) and ___ Little Miss Library case(s) at £5.49 each.

❏ **3.** Please enrol the following in the Mr Men & Little Miss Club at £10.72 (inc postage)

Fan's Name:_____Fan's Address:_____

_____Post Code:_____Date of birth:___/___/___

Your Name:_____Your Address:_____

_____

Post Code:_____Name of parent or guardian (if not you):_____

Total amount due: £_____ (£5.49 per Library Case, £10.72 per Club membership)

❏ I enclose a cheque or postal order payable to Egmont World Limited.

❏ Please charge my MasterCard / Visa account.

Card number: | | | | | | | | | | | | | | | | |

Expiry Date: _____/_____   Signature: _____

Data Protection Act: If you do **not** wish to receive other family offers from us or companies we recommend, please tick this box ❏. Offer applies to UK only

3 Great Offers For Mr Men Fans

1 Token EGMONT WORLD

1 FREE Door Hangers and Posters

In every Mr Men and Little Miss Book like this one you will find a special token. Collect 6 and we will send you either a brilliant Mr. Men or Little Miss poster and a Mr Men or Little Miss double sided, full colour, bedroom door hanger. Apply using the coupon overleaf, enclosing six tokens and a 50p coin for your choice of two items.

Egmont World tokens can be used towards any other Egmont World / World International token scheme promotions., in early learning and story / activity books.

Posters: Tick your preferred choice of either Mr Men ☐ or Little Miss ☐

Door Hangers: Choose from: Mr. Nosey & Mr Muddle ☐, Mr Greedy & Mr Lazy ☐, Mr Tickle & Mr Grumpy ☐, Mr Slow & Mr Busy ☐, Mr Messy & Mr Quiet ☐, Mr Perfect & Mr Forgetful ☐, Little Miss Fun & Little Miss Late ☐, Little Miss Helpful & Little Miss Tidy ☐, Little Miss Busy & Little Miss Brainy ☐, Little Miss Star & Little Miss Fun ☐. (Please tick)

ENTRANCE FEE 3 SAUSAGES

2 Mr Men Library Boxes

Keep your growing collection of Mr Men and Little Miss books in these superb library boxes. With an integral carrying handle and stay-closed fastener, these full colour, plastic boxes are fantastic. They are just £5.49 each including postage. Order overleaf.

3 Join The Club

To join the fantastic Mr Men & Little Miss Club, check out the page overleaf NOW!

Allow 28 days for delivery. We reserve the right to change the terms of this offer at any time but we offer a 14 day money back guarantee. The money-back guarantee does not affect your statutory rights. Birthday and Christmas cards are sent care of parent/guardians in advance of the day. After 31/12/00 please call to check that the offer details are still correct.

MR MEN and LITTLE MISS™ & © 1998 Mrs. Roger Hargreaves